# The Islander

# The Islander

*a novel by*

# Cynthia Rylant

**A YEARLING BOOK**

Published by
Bantam Doubleday Dell Books for Young Readers
a division of
Random House, Inc.
1540 Broadway
New York, New York 10036

The trademarks Yearling® and Dell® are registered in the U.S. Patent and Trademark Office and in other countries.

Visit us on the Web! www.randomhouse.com

Educators and librarians, for a variety of teaching tools, visit us at
www.randomhouse.com/teachers

ISBN: 0-440-41542-X

Reprinted by arrangement with DK Publishing, Inc.

Printed in the United States of America

December 1999

10 9 8 7

OPM

# The Islander

*My name is Daniel Jennings, and on this day, my twentieth birthday, I wish to make a record of the marvelous things that happened to me when I was a boy.*

*I dedicate it to my grandfather.*

# Part One

# The Mermaid

# ONE

I was a boy when I met the mermaid, and, of course, no one believed me. It didn't matter. I was a solitary boy—lonely, actually—and had long given up on anyone understanding what I said or how I felt. I had lived with my grandfather for three years, and he was a kind and gentle man, but he could not see into a boy's world and so could not do much more than love me.

The mermaid must have known that she could trust me. She must have known I had only a grandfather who taught me to read and write and then left me to my own education as he returned to the alder wood he carved for a living.

And read I did, every day and sometimes all night long, and I knew things most boys didn't know and was ignorant of things most boys are sure of. I knew why heroes sometimes fall and why wise men sometimes do terrible things and where in the world one might actually get a glimpse of heaven. But I could not multiply by seven and did not guess, ever, that stars had names.

I lived on an island called Coquille off the coast of British Columbia. There was no electricity, and visitors were rare. Perhaps thirty families lived on the entire island, and they mostly kept to themselves. Island people are exactly that. Islands. The larger world does not interest them.

But it interested me. Oh, how it interested me. I longed for the simplest pleasures. To ride a horse (I had never even seen one). To take a train. To drive on long open roads forever and never meet the water's edge. I wanted to know what I was missing. What was happening in the world without me.

And I thought I might never know. Until

one evening, in the light of a full moon, someone spoke my name.

And the whole wide world opened.

# TWO

The mermaid was shy, like me. I had always been shy. My grandfather was forever reminding me to speak louder, hold my head up, shake hands with a strong, firm grip.

Not that there were many opportunities to practice this. I saw other islanders rarely. I did not attend school with the children of Coquille, for they had to be boated to a larger island each day, and Grandfather would not allow me on the water without him. We went to church on occasional Sundays, and met the docking of the mainland ferry on Thursdays. But most days I could get by with speaking softly and holding my head however I chose, which was usually low to the ground so I could find interesting things to put in my pocket.

And it was this habit of bad posture that actually brought me to the mermaid.

Living by the ocean, I hardly noticed it. The sea spread out blue and wide before me each day, but I didn't care. I wanted small things to take home, so the cliffs, the fields, the shore at low tide were what interested me. I collected rocks, glass, shells, bones, feathers. I loved finding coins. And, of course, I always hoped for a letter in a bottle. What boy doesn't? A letter from a young girl in China—a princess, perhaps—who needed someone's help.

And I would write back to her, but instead of sending the bottle (which might be lost), I would give the letter to a wise gull, instructing it to find the girl in China and bring me back her reply.

This way, I imagined, I might find a friend.

So it was, with my head full of dreams like these and my eyes on the ground, that one afternoon I stumbled across something that made me gasp and stop and literally rub my eyes with wonder. And when I was certain I wasn't imagining the thing that lay before me, I stooped and picked it up.

It was a mermaid's comb. I knew it was a mermaid's comb because, as I have said, mine was an unusual education. One of the many volumes in my grandfather's library was a book on sea lore, and in it a chapter on sea people. I had read this chapter at least a dozen times, for not being able to find a true friend on land, I had imagined finding one in the sea. But I really didn't expect such a thing to happen. I was a wisher, it is true, but my wishes were practical and involved things like bus tickets and horse ranches.

I had not wished for a mermaid.

But I knew, when I saw the comb that day, exactly what it was. For it was, amazingly, a living thing. Like the starfish that clings to the rocks and the coral that sways in the seas, the comb was alive.

And so beautiful. It glinted green and blue and silver in the sun, the outer rim of it hard like a shell, but its teeth soft and alive, like the tentacles of a jellyfish. And in my hands it vibrated like the tuning fork on my grand-father's mantel.

I had discovered a mermaid's comb. The possibilities of what might happen next made my head swim.

So I sat down and breathed deeply as my eyes looked out across the vast blue water.

The sea was finally interesting to me. I stared at it for a very, very long time.

# THREE

I decided after what seemed many hours to wait right there for the mermaid to come back. The sun had set, and the tide was coming in. I knew the rocks where I'd found the comb would soon be covered with water, so I climbed farther up the bank and found a soft spot in the sea grasses to wait. I was concerned about my grandfather, who would be worrying about me when I did not come home for supper. But how many chances does one have to find a mermaid?

It was a beautiful night filled with stars and the full moon. I sat in the grasses and thought of my parents, both dead, and wondered if they flew among the stars, holding hands. In my mind I called out to them and hoped they could see me from wherever they were. I wondered if they would recognize me now.

The night was chilly, but living on the island I'd learned always to keep a jacket around my waist for unexpected rains or sudden cold storms. So I pulled it on and was content. My hands lightly stroked the mermaid's comb, and its teeth tickled my fingers. The comb felt warm, and, oddly, happy to me.

Boys can sit quite still when they have to and are always better able to hide themselves than grown people. Perhaps it is because I was so good at this that the mermaid came swimming toward the rocks, free of caution or fear.

When I realized what was actually in the water, heading my way, my heart pounded so that I was afraid for a moment I might die. It is one thing to read of mermaids or angels or fairy people. It is another to be all alone in witness of such. I felt cold and faint and sick.

Then suddenly the comb in my hand began to move. Not just quiver but in fact to move as if it were trying to stand on end or rise up out of my hands and fly. And I became so involved in holding on to it that I did not see the mermaid swim past the rocks to the edge of the sand and somehow settle herself out of water, near the grasses where I was hiding and holding desperately to her comb.

But then I heard a soft whistle and, looking up, I saw her not more than twenty feet away. I froze. The comb slipped from my fingers and floated through the air until she caught it and slid it into her hair. And we sat in silence, each knowing the other was there.

Then she spoke my name.

"Daniel."

And her voice was so beautiful and familiar that all my fear left me and I could not stop myself from answering.

"Yes."

And when I spoke, the mermaid slipped back down to the sea and was gone.

I told you she was shy.

# FOUR

My grandfather's cottage was built by his grandfather from stones and boulders gathered from the shore, and the sense of time and the elements was everywhere in it. I could feel, some nights, the comforting presence of all who had lived there before, and this gave me the feeling of being part of a very large family. Water buckets a hundred years old still stood by the back door. And a child named

Anna had carved her name in a beam above my attic bed. I was sorry Anna was not still here, for I so longed to tell someone about the mermaid who would believe me. I felt Anna would.

Grandfather was justly angry with me when finally I arrived at the cottage past midnight, the evening of the mermaid. He had been out with his lantern, calling and calling, and the fear was still in his eyes though I was home and safe. And I do not know whether it was because he was so upset and I pitied him, or whether I simply could not lie about the most important night of my life, but I told him the truth. I told him I had found a mermaid.

And his fussing and scolding stopped.

He looked at me, long, and when he finally spoke it was not with anger or judgment.

He simply said, softly, "It's all right, son."

And because I was wise in certain ways, I knew exactly what he was feeling. I knew that my grandfather believed I was not well, that my mind was not well, and that the loss of my parents and the loneliness of living with him had made me so.

If I had told him that I'd spent the evening with my foot stuck between two logs, or that I'd been cornered by a bear, or that I'd fallen asleep in the sea grasses, he would have been relieved by my slippery story. He would have guessed that I was simply having too good a time somewhere to want to come home and that, like an ordinary boy, I was trying to fib my way out of trouble.

But when I told him I'd seen a mermaid—and I *couldn't* bring myself to say anything else—I believe he felt he'd truly lost me. I could see it by the hand across his forehead, his troubled eyes.

And I wanted to take back what I'd told him. I wanted to wash away the mermaid story and come up with some other kind of story, something really clever and naughty and normal.

But it was too late. And there was nothing for me to do but go to bed and pray that my grandfather still loved me and that the mermaid would come back.

Because I couldn't give her up altogether. Seeing her that evening made me believe in things I'd never believed in before. And for the first time, I felt a part of the world. For the world was no longer little stone houses and wooden boats and the cry of gulls at dawn. It was larger and deeper and more marvelous than I had ever known, and being absolutely sure of this made me want, more than ever, to be alive.

Of course, I could not possibly sit in the grasses and wait late into the night ever again. Given the anguish I'd already caused my grandfather, I could not bring myself to disobey him. Not even for the miracle of a mermaid.

But I felt she would surely return to those rocks. So I borrowed an idea from an old dream of mine, and I put a letter in a bottle. This is what it said:

> *Dear Mermaid,*
> *Please find me.*
> *Daniel*

I put the bottle on the same rock where I had discovered her comb.

And I waited.

# FIVE

The bottle disappeared with the tide, and I found myself thinking of nothing else. In the days of waiting for an answer to my letter, I would catch myself repeating the whistle I had heard from the mermaid's lips or moving my fingers over the teeth of an imaginary comb. At night my dreams were full of salt water and searching, and I would wake, suddenly, and think of her.

Then finally, on the ninth day, something happened.

I had gone to the rocks each morning and each evening, hoping to see the mermaid again or to hear from her somehow. I had little hope she would come to the rocks before dark, so instead I looked far out on the water for any sign she might be there. In eight days I'd seen nothing.

But on the ninth day, as the sun lay low on the horizon and the water glistened orange and gold, washing around the rocks where I waited, a sea otter suddenly bobbed up almost beside me. Otters were a common sight near the island's shore—I saw them often—so at first I was just disappointed that the creature in the water was not the mermaid, then disinterested that it was an otter.

But something extraordinary happened.

The otter was swimming with a shell in its paws—as otters often do—when suddenly it gave three short barks and one long one. The rhythm was so startling that I turned toward the sound.

And as I looked more closely at the otter, I noticed that it had on its forehead a very unusual marking: a large white diamond.

Then, as I leaned more curiously forward, the otter tossed its shell to me and disappeared into the waves.

Holding that shell in my hands, I knew, of

course, that again the marvelous was happening. And again I felt that cold fear when one is faced with something mysterious and unknown. Both happiness and dread ran through me.

I used my pocketknife to pry open the shell. And inside I found a key.

It was small, ornate, and very old. Its brass had tarnished to black. I had no idea what it meant nor what to do with it. But I knew—I was absolutely *certain*—that the mermaid had sent it, and I was so moved that I nearly wept.

I could not remember ever feeling so important.

That evening, with a candle beside my bed,

I wrote another letter. This one read:

> Dear Mermaid,
>   The key is beautiful. What
> does it open?
>   I miss you.
>
>               Daniel

I left the bottle for her very early the next morning, as the tide was still pulling from the shore, and I believed that somehow I would hear from her again.

And the story of that is even more marvelous than what I have just told.

*Part Two*

# The Key

# SIX

Two weeks later our island was hit by a great storm.

We had been warned it was coming, and of course we knew—without the warning—that terrible weather was on its way. A hard wind had whipped sand into the forests for two days, and fishermen had already lashed their small boats to the docks and turned their backs to the sea.

My grandfather had lived through a hurricane as a boy, and because of it he had a deep fear and an abiding respect for the wind. And he had always kept, as his father had before him, a tiny cellar beneath the cottage stocked with water, food, blankets, and lanterns. It was here, on the third day of the storm, that we stayed.

In the time since receiving the mysterious key, I had had no messages from the mermaid, no signs of her anywhere. Strangely, this did not trouble me. From the moment I'd been given the key I had begun to feel a sense of calm such as I had never felt before. Whatever small things that may have worried me in the pást, these no longer mattered. And because of this I believed there was a good reason the mermaid had disappeared and that she would one day find me again.

The storm, when it came, was as good a reason for disappearing as any on earth. Or sea.

In the cellar my grandfather wrapped blankets around me and we sat on an old bench against the cold dirt wall, his large, veined hand on mine, and we listened.

"Grandfather," I said, "will it blow away our house?"

"No, son, the stones are too heavy. The house will stand."

"Will it blow away the trees?"

"Some," he answered.

"And the birds in the trees?"

"Yes."

I sat still and listened again.

"Grandfather, what will happen to the fish in the sea?"

He began to answer me when all at once the wind roared against his voice and over everything above us, and we could hear all manner of destruction—objects thudding against the house, the long loud moan of hundred-year-old rafters, the small kitchen above us shaking, and the clatter of pans and bowls knocking to the floor. Grandfather put his arm around me and I shut my eyes tight and we sat this way for a long time.

Then finally it was quiet, and we went out to see what remained.

Our cottage had held, though part of its roof was missing and much of the inside was saturated from the rains. Still, it had held, and we were not without a home.

By now the sun had risen and we could see to make our way across the island to those who might need our help. Grandfather brought medicine and bandages, a jug of clean water, rope, matches, and an ax.

I carried two blankets, rolled up with string.

I have never forgotten the world we discovered that morning. The immense sadness left behind, the splintered trees, the silent birds, the small houses torn to pieces.

We did what we could.

We walked first to our nearest neighbors. Luckily no one had died. But the man had suffered a blow to the head and was laid out on the ground, a coat across him, his wife by his side. Grandfather knelt down and looked in his eyes. The man was still conscious.

"Keep him awake if you can," Grandfather told the man's wife. "He mustn't sleep for several hours. If you do this, I think he will be all right."

I could see that the woman believed every word my grandfather said and would do exactly as he told her.

We moved from home to home through the day, my grandfather tending the ill, surveying the damage, offering counsel to young families whose first terrible storm this was.

And as the hours passed, color eventually began to return to the islanders' stricken faces. And a feeling of joy at just being alive floated in the air. The sun shone bright and the sky was a sharp crystal blue and, by afternoon, even birds flew again.

"What of the sea gulls?" I asked my grandfather after he had helped cut a tree away from a family's front door. "And the sea lions?"

Grandfather gave a deep sigh.

"There will be animals on the shore today that didn't survive the storm. And more will be washed up."

Suddenly my mind whirled. I thought of

the otter, the rocks, the key, the comb, and of her.

"Is it all right if I go there?" I asked. "Maybe I can save . . ."

I didn't know what I might save. I shrugged my shoulders and looked at him.

Grandfather studied my face.

"You may go, Daniel," he finally said, "to search the shore. But you must promise me you'll return home within the hour."

I nodded.

"There will be little you can do," he added quietly. "But if you find a creature you think we might save, bring it back in a blanket. We'll see then."

38

We parted, Grandfather turning to walk to the next house on the island, me turning toward the sea.

Around my neck, beneath my shirt, hung the mermaid's key.

# SEVEN

I was ten years old when I walked the shore after that storm, and I had been an orphan for three years. My parents' small plane had gone down into the sea, and it was never recovered. And because I did not ever see them dead, I think that I never completely believed they were. Death had not convinced me.

But after the storm, stepping over the bodies

of so many lifeless gulls, puffins, sandpipers, plovers, and even two small sea lions, I finally believed in death, and for the first time, I was certain my parents were never coming back.

It is too sad to say how it all looked. I did not know what to do with each lifeless creature I came upon. So I simply knelt down and placed my hand on each one that I found, then walked on.

I thought, when I first arrived at the beach, that I had come to look for the mermaid. I had been afraid for her, afraid she, too, had been thrown lifeless onto the sand.

But as I walked and looked and understood, I did not worry for her at all. For I knew that the creatures that lay all around me were as real and mortal as I. I understood their frail bodies, their small beating hearts suddenly silenced. And I knew, somehow, that she was not one of them. She was not one of us.

I resolved to find at least one living creature that I might save before returning to my grandfather. Even if I had to stay longer than promised.

I found two.

I had been walking for perhaps thirty minutes when I neared a large mass of driftwood, seaweed, and rocks, and as I drew closer, a startling thing occurred.

The key hanging around my neck began to

vibrate. Just as the comb in my hand had vibrated many days before.

With each step I took toward the pile of debris, I felt the vibrations stronger against my chest. Putting my hand over the key, I stopped and listened.

And I heard something stir under a large piece of driftwood.

I stepped carefully onto a boulder so I might get a closer look beneath the log.

I found a pelican. Alive.

It was stunned, and its eyes were closed, but with the last bit of strength it possessed, it was trying to flap its tired wings and free itself.

I unrolled one of the blankets I was carrying

and carefully laid it over the bird. Then gently I picked it up, soothing it with my voice, and I fashioned the blanket into a large pouch tied at the top so I might better carry the poor fellow home.

The bird's struggling quieted, and it seemed content to go with me.

I walked perhaps another thirty or forty minutes along the shore, looking for any other creature I might carry home. I felt certain Grandfather could save anything I might find. But I saw no others, and the key around my neck no longer vibrated.

Then, just as I began to turn back, the key moved again. And with each step I took, the stronger its motion became.

And I found, beneath a heavy mass of sea-weed, another pelican, still breathing.

This one I wrapped into the other blanket.

I carried the birds home, and when Grand-father finally returned, I did not tell him about the key, nor did I speak of the dead creatures I had witnessed.

I simply led him to the closet where I'd settled the pelicans together on an old coat on the floor. I helped him lift them out, and I watched as he carefully splinted the wing of one and medicated the injured eye and leg of the other. Then we settled them again to rest.

Closing the closet door, Grandfather smiled at me.

"You're a good boy, Daniel."

And at that moment something changed between us. I felt, almost, like a son.

Instinctively I placed my hand over the hidden key.

# EIGHT

My grandfather and I spent the remaining weeks of that fall helping to restore our small island. We rebuilt walls and fences. We helped patch roofs and boats. We carried rocks and logs and buckets of clay. And in this time another surprising thing occurred.

I became an islander.

I learned the names of many of the families who lived in the small houses of Coquille. Young husbands and wives, grandparents, babies, children. Many learned my name and came to know me well enough to tease me affectionately or pat me on the shoulder or rub their knuckles softly on my head.

I still found no one my own age whom I could call a real friend. But I found a community.

And I discovered another thing: that I had a gift with birds.

The two pelicans I brought home after the storm were not the last birds my grandfather and I nursed back to health. Every several days or so I would be out somewhere on the island,

and suddenly I would feel the mermaid's key vibrate against my chest. I would stop and listen, and sure enough, I would find an injured bird, hiding in the grasses or shivering in a bush.

Soon it became apparent to my grandfather and me that we were going to run out of closet space if I continued coming home with plovers and sea gulls wrapped in my jacket.

So together we built an aviary out of lumber and chicken wire, and we made nests and cages from lobster traps and netting, and we found ourselves with a small bird sanctuary.

And very soon I learned that I could calm a distressed gull with my voice, could touch a puffin and convince it to trust me, could splint and bandage and clean any sort of winged creature I found—and do it well.

Always it was the mermaid's key which would lead me to these creatures that needed my help. The key vibrated no other time than when it alerted me to an injured bird. And I began to think that this was the key's only purpose.

I was wrong.

In early winter the wind turned cold and the rains began, and all the islanders moved indoors to their heavy sweaters and warm fires. I saw less and less of our neighbors as Grandfather and I spent more time reading or warming a sick bird by the stove.

Then one evening, during an especially hard rain, there came a sudden loud banging on our door. I put down my book and, alarmed, followed Grandfather to see who was there.

It was David Mills, who lived perhaps ten miles from us.

"The Buchmans have lost their little girl," he said, gasping, the rain dripping off the hood of his jacket and onto his face.

"She wandered off, and it's been four hours and no sign of her. They need people to help search."

Grandfather rushed to get our coats and boots and lanterns, and within minutes we were out the door and in the cab of Mr. Mills's truck.

Grandfather and I did not know the Buchmans well, for they lived at the farther tip of the island, and we could not remember their child. But she was, we learned, only five years old. She had been on the porch after supper, watching the rain, and in the time it took her mother to go inside and pull a cake from the oven, the child was gone.

Now it was nearing ten o'clock. The temperature was dropping, the rain was turning to sleet, and the forests were completely dark.

A panic moved across the island.

Everyone had headed out with flashlights, lanterns, dogs. How far could a little child wander in four hours? And in what direction?

Toward the sea and its cliffs, or deep into the woods that extended for miles?

When we arrived at the Buchman house, we could see small reflections of lanterns moving in the surrounding trees. Mrs. Buchman stood on the porch, her hand across her mouth, her face tight and anxious.

Grandfather and I jumped out of the truck.

"Should we split up?" I asked him.

He thought a moment.

"No, let's stay together," he said. "We don't need two lost children tonight."

He looked toward an area of the woods that was not yet lit with searchers.

"We'll head there," he said.

53

We began walking. It was slow going, for there was no moon that evening to help light the way, and the firs stood thick in our path. The big storm at summer's end had left fallen trees and branches everywhere, and picking our way around these was very difficult.

Unless the child called out and was heard, it seemed impossible anyone would find her, at least not until daylight. And the night was getting colder.

I don't know how long Grandfather and I had been searching—perhaps an hour or more—when suddenly something familiar occurred.

The key I wore began to vibrate.

I put my hand to my chest.

"Grandfather," I said, "she's near here."

Grandfather raised his lantern to my face.

"How do you know?" he asked.

"I just know," I said. I had never told him about the key. I had decided never to tell anyone. "She's here," I repeated.

I turned and made my way a few steps to the left. The vibration grew weaker. I turned in the opposite direction. As I walked, the key's movement grew strong.

"She's here," I said again. "I'm sure of it."

I stepped carefully over logs and branches, around thick undergrowth and through heavy ferns. Grandfather was following me.

Now the key vibrated so strongly I could almost feel it echo through my chest. I stopped and carefully swung my lantern in a slow circle.

And there, beneath some bushes at the base of a rotting pine, was the girl. Her eyes were closed.

"Oh my heaven," I heard my grandfather say.

I held both lanterns as he lifted her up in his arms. The child's lips were blue.

"Hypothermia," said Grandfather. "We have to get her back, quickly."

He removed his coat and wrapped it around her.

"Grandfather, you'll be sick," I said.

"I'll be fine," he answered. "Hurry!"

And we did. We got the child home, where the local nurse was waiting, and as Grandfather and I stood at the end of the bed, we watched as she tended the girl. Mr. and Mrs. Buchman were at either side, tears on their faces.

After a short while, the little girl regained consciousness. Slowly opening her eyes, she looked at her mother's face, then her father's face, and she smiled.

Finally she looked at me at the end of the bed.

And as I stared back at those large, wondering eyes, I believe I knew, even then, that one day this girl was going to mean something to me.

*Part Three*

# The Photograph

# NINE

And now time must pass, in my telling, to the year I was seventeen.

During the days of my growing from a boy of ten into a young man, there was always a certain feeling of enchantment in my life. But in these years I never again experienced anything as magical as when I met the mermaid.

I did not see her a second time, nor any sign of her, and had I not worn her key around my neck, I might not have believed in her at all. I might have convinced myself that I had just fallen asleep there in the sea grasses and had merely dreamed her. I might have told myself the comb was just some sort of rare sea life that had been plucked away as I slept and that carried no real magic at all.

But the key I wore was, without a doubt, pure magic. It had saved a child's life one night. It had saved, and continued to save, countless birds. And I had nothing to do with this power. The key's wonderful knowing was all its own, and I could only be grateful for the privilege of having it.

I never removed the key from my neck. Ever. I cherished and protected it every moment of my life.

At night I would lie in bed, holding the key in my palm, and I would think. Always this relaxed me. I would look toward the moon shining in the open window or stare at the beam where Anna had once carved her name, and I would consider my life—what I had lost and gained, what I hoped for.

And always I felt that something truly extraordinary would happen to me again someday. I could not guess what it might be. But I always had an almost giddy sense of anticipation, much like the feeling I'd had when I was ten and found the mermaid's comb.

For seven years my life had been filled with quiet routine and contentment. I continued to read and to educate myself (a library on the mainland sent me books by ferry). I had a fascination with geography, with history. But I had no plans to pursue a formal education. My grandfather's love of carving was, I discovered, in my blood as well, and I hoped to follow his path in this.

Grandfather's work sold well in the coastal galleries, and there was always someone on the ferry every few months, looking to pick up a new collection.

So I carved, studied, and I waited—waited for the future to tell me why my heart was so *ready*.

Then, on April sixteenth of that year, my grandfather and I began the day by releasing a strong, healthy cormorant into the sky. And in the evening of the same day, my grandfather died.

He had not been ill and there had been no signs that he might suddenly die. He simply finished the day like any other, then lay down his head and passed into heaven.

The day following the funeral was especially hard for me. The sorrow was hard. Throughout the morning and afternoon, one islander after another stopped by to see how I was, to tell me how much my grandfather would be missed. And each time someone came and went, the lonelier I felt.

In the evening I decided I would sort through the things Grandfather had left behind. In this way I thought I might feel him still with me.

I opened the small desk in his bedroom and organized the few letters and bills I found there. I looked through a drawer of broken watches. I sharpened his pencils.

I then moved to Grandfather's bureau to see if there might be a piece of his clothing—a sweater perhaps—I could wear in memory of him. And as I lifted out a few of the old flannel shirts lying in the top drawer, I came across a worn brown Bible tied with a thin piece of silk ribbon.

Sitting down on Grandfather's bed, I carefully untied the silk. The need of it was apparent, for several of the delicate yellowed pages were loose.

I opened the cover and read: "To my son, Andrew Michael Jennings, on your sixth birthday. Love, Mother."

I did not know who Andrew Jennings was, but on the next page was a family tree, and I saw that he was my great-grandfather. My grandfather's name, his son, was directly below it.

Alongside Grandfather's name was another, the name of a sister: Anna Elizabeth.

*Anna.*

I smiled. The child in the attic had been my grandfather's sister. But he had not ever spoken of her.

Beneath Grandfather's name was my father's—Ethan.

And beneath my father's name was my own.

But there were no names beneath Anna Elizabeth's.

Carefully I paged through Grandfather's Bible for other revelations. A thin lace handkerchief slid out. And a torn piece of music—it seemed part of an old hymn. Then a dried rose.

And, last, a very old photograph.

It was a picture of a young woman, probably in her teens, sitting on a carved wooden chair with a dog at her side.

I looked closely at the girl's face. She was beautiful, with kind eyes and thick dark hair flowing to her waist.

My gaze then turned to the dog.

And my heart stopped.

For there, on the dog's forehead, I could see a very unusual marking:

A large white diamond.

Certain I was dreaming, I turned the photograph over.

Written was this:

"Anna Elizabeth"
Born 1898   Died 1915

# TEN

Only one person from my grandfather's youth was, as far as I knew, still alive, and her name was Hester Maxwell. She lived in a house on the mainland, and I had met her years ago on one of my rare trips off the island. Grandfather had carved an orca for her eighty-fifth birthday, and one morning we had crossed on the ferry to her home, shared lunch, then returned. I would likely not have remembered where she lived except that it was beside a taffy shop, which was, of course, very interesting to me. Grandfather bought several pieces for us.

If anyone could tell me anything about Anna, it would be Mrs. Maxwell. So, two weeks after my grandfather's passing, I carried his Bible across the water to the door of her house.

You must guess that by now I completely believed that the mermaid who had come to me so many years before was Anna, the young woman in the photograph. The face of Anna's dog and the face of the otter that had brought the key were too astonishingly alike for me to believe anything else.

And realizing this, I was filled with a combination of the most awful anxiety and incredible joy.

I was anxious because I now believed that the mermaid who had visited me was a *ghost*. And the thought of ghosts makes (and has always made) me anxious.

But with this I also felt a profound happiness. Magic is one thing. And it is a marvelous thing.

But an everlasting spirit is even more.

I needed to know who Anna had been.

Mrs. Maxwell was quite frail, but she remembered me right away and invited me

inside. She had not been told of my grandfather's death, and I was sorry to tell her. But
she was surprisingly calm at the news. Perhaps in old age, death becomes a promise. A
good one.

After a cup of tea I unwrapped the Bible in
my hands and slipped out Anna's photograph.
I handed it to Mrs. Maxwell.

"I found this in Grandfather's Bible," I said.
"I wonder if you remember her. I believe she
was his sister."

Mrs. Maxwell gently took the photograph
from my hands and carefully brought it up
near her eyes. Then, all at once, she began
to cry.

I jumped up and fetched some tissues for her

from a nearby table. I sat quietly while she dried her wrinkled eyes, all the while murmuring, "Forgive me."

Finally she could speak. She handed the photograph back to me and said, softly, "When I was growing up on Coquille, Anna was my dearest friend. I thought I would die after we lost her."

"Lost her?" I asked. "How?"

Mrs. Maxwell smiled, but her eyes grew moist again.

"Anna loved her dog," she answered. "More than anything in the world. I've never seen a person so in love with an animal."

She sighed deeply, then continued.

"There was a very bad storm one night. Very bad. Many boats were lost.

"Anna and the dog had gone to the shore to look for her father, who was a fisherman. He'd left that morning and by nightfall hadn't come home.

"The winds were very bad. Everyone was worried.

"So Anna went searching for her father. She climbed with her dog to the top of a sea stack, hoping to see her father's boat. Someone saw her there and warned her, tried to get her to come down.

"But she wouldn't. She stood there, with the dog, looking out at the black sea."

Mrs. Maxwell stopped again. She took two deep breaths.

"A large wave rolled over that rock and swept Anna's dog into the water. The poor thing went under immediately. The water was terrible that night. Anna screamed and called the dog's name. She called and called. But he did not surface. And then Anna dove in."

Mrs. Maxwell put her small thin hand to her heart.

"They were both lost," she whispered.

I felt the warm sting of tears behind my eyes.

"How old was she?" I asked.

"She was exactly your age," said Mrs. Maxwell. "Seventeen. She was the loveliest . . ." Mrs. Maxwell shook her head.

"And Anna's father? His boat?" I asked.

"He'd taken shelter in a cove for the night and came home the next day.

"Your grandfather was just a boy, only twelve, when his sister perished. He'd always been so happy, so outgoing. Ever afterward, he was quiet."

Now it was I who sighed deeply, sadly.

Mrs. Maxwell looked at me, then placed her warm hand over mine.

"I am so sorry, my dear," she said, "that you have lost everyone."

I lifted my head and looked at her in surprise.

Unbelievably, until that moment, I didn't realize I had.

*Part Four*

# The Islander

# ELEVEN

In the weeks following my grandfather's death, people were very kind to me. The women brought me casseroles and cakes, the men stopped by to see whether I needed anything. Children were sent to invite me to supper.

It is a grace that comes, unexpected, after tragedy—this reminder that most hearts are good.

Grandfather had left a substantial savings behind, an amount that surprised me, given his simple way of life. So I did not fear poverty.

What I feared was loneliness. And in spite of the islanders' best efforts, my loneliness was overwhelming. Though not social by any means, I did enjoy the comfort of family. Grandfather had been my family, and I missed the quiet routine of our life—a pot of coffee shared on the front steps in summer or near the wood stove in winter. The steady rhythm of two carving knives. The good smell of stew.

As a young boy I had been lonely, isolated. I was too young then to appreciate the friend my grandfather might be.

But growing up, in caring for birds, learning to carve, sharing the work around the cottage, I had truly learned to love my grandfather as a friend, and I had nearly forgotten what loneliness felt like.

With Grandfather gone, I seemed unable to accomplish anything. When we'd released the cormorant on the day he died, there had been no other birds left to tend. And since then, I had found no new birds. In fact I had not been to the shore at all. I stayed inside the house. Sometimes I just sat, for hours. Or I slept. I slept quite a bit.

This went on for nearly three months. And although my refrigerator was well stocked with frozen casseroles, I lost weight. I felt so weak, so tired.

Then one night I became very ill. I lay in bed, my body burning with fever, my head spinning, my fingers numb. I retched and vomited and coughed until tears came. I had never, ever been so sick.

And because I was so sick and weak and without anyone, all my emotions overcame me, and I found myself sobbing.

Trembling, with my hand on the key around my neck, I stared up at the beam where Anna had carved her name.

And I whispered, "Anna, please help me."

I cried for a time, then finally fell into sleep.

I slept for eighteen hours and did not wake until suppertime the next day.

But when I woke, I felt fine. All traces of illness were gone, and I was clear-headed and ravenously hungry.

I put together a huge meal for myself, a smorgasbord from all the ladies' kindnesses in my refrigerator. And I ate and ate and ate.

Then when I was finished, I felt an urge to do something I hadn't done in a while.

I wanted to walk the shore.

Already it was nightfall, but the moon was full and there was enough light for me to find my way among the rocks and grasses. I breathed deeply the fresh air, the scents of seaweed and shells. I believe I loved the ocean more that night than any other night of my life.

I was moving along, watching the waves and the moon and the stars coming out in the sky one by one, when something else happened that had not occurred in a while.

The key around my neck began to vibrate.

I placed my hand over it, then stopped and listened. The surf was so loud that it was difficult to hear much else.

But I did hear something. A cry of some sort. And a scraping.

I followed the direction of the sound, and about twenty feet away, wedged between two large pieces of driftwood, I discovered a wooden box. Inside it, something was definitely alive.

The key pulsed strongly now, warming my chest as I moved my hands over the box. The crying inside had stopped, but the scraping noise continued.

I tried to lift the hinged lid, but it wouldn't move. There was a lock holding it shut.

I pulled and pulled at this lock, trying to force it open with my hands. But it was too sturdy.

Then a thought came to me.

For the first time since I'd hung it around my neck seven years before, I removed the mermaid's key. I put it into the lock. And the lock opened.

Carefully I lifted up the lid only an inch or so. I was worried what might fly out at me.

But I didn't worry long. For a small smooth tongue licked the tips of my fingers, and a cold wet nose nudged the palm of my hand.

In the box was a puppy.

And he became my family.

# TWELVE

**M**y dog's name is Poseidon, after the god of the sea. He's large now and brown, with floppy ears and big paws and a nose for puffins.

Yes, puffins. And gulls and auklets and murres. Poseidon finds injured seabirds long before I do, long before the key vibrates. In fact, since he is finding them first, the key has stopped moving altogether. It seems to know that its work is done.

I have had Poseidon for three years. When I brought him home that first night, after rescuing him from the box, he crawled into bed with me and laid his head beside my feet and snored like a chain saw. We still sleep this way.

He loves to play as much now as when he was a puppy. He especially loves to retrieve, and I can throw anything anywhere and he will find it.

And he loves the birds in the same way I do. When we carry home a gull with a broken wing, Poseidon will walk close beside me, sniffing the bird, his eyes full of concern. And while I am setting the bird's wing or dressing a wound, Poseidon will lick the bird's face. The birds have never minded.

Poseidon travels with me on the ferry when I take my carvings to the mainland. He's a great friend of the ferry captain, who has taken to keeping a tin of biscuits in his cabin just for Poseidon.

I'm proud to have continued my grandfather's tradition with my carvings, though I will likely never be the craftsman he was. Still, I will keep trying.

Mrs. Maxwell is still alive and in remarkably good health for someone who is ninety-three years old. Poseidon and I stop and see her when we are nearby, and I bring her tea and chocolates, which she likes very much. Mrs. Maxwell has become a sort of aunt to me.

In addition to carving, and keeping birds, and playing with Poseidon, I've taken up one more activity.

I've joined the church choir.

I have no voice and can barely carry a tune and at times I feel a little more than silly in those long robes.

But this is the only way I can see Franny, who sings in the choir as well.

Franny is only fifteen, so I feel it wouldn't be proper to court her just yet. I am patient to wait a few more years, provided no one else tries to marry her.

She's a lovely girl with large brown eyes and a beautiful singing voice, and I know there will be plenty of boys who will want her for their own.

But I have one advantage over all of them: I once saved her life.

Yes, Franny is—or was—the small girl Grandfather and I found in the cold woods that night ten years ago. And one day I hope to marry her. She seems to like me very much, so I think I have a chance.

One evening last week after choir practice, Franny and I took a walk with Poseidon along the shore. The sun was setting and spreading orange and silver over the dark green water. The island was beautiful.

Franny and I talked and talked about our hopes, our secret wishes, those things we wanted to be and do in our lives (Franny hopes to be a painter). As we talked, the breeze blew Franny's long hair softly against her face and I could hardly stop looking at her. Poseidon wanted to retrieve, so she threw a bit of driftwood for him again and again, laughing at his funny ways.

It was a remarkable evening.

After I walked Franny home, I biked with Poseidon beside me back to our little cottage.

And I felt so happy, so filled with good hope. I had finally let go the desire I'd had as a boy to see the larger world, and I knew I would be content to be an islander for the rest of my life.

I had found in Poseidon, in Mrs. Maxwell, and now in Franny, what I had longed for since my grandfather's death: a family.

And I had found them because of the mermaid.

Though I know her name, I also know that I will never understand the mystery of her. I cannot begin to guess where our spirits might dwell once we have left this sweet earth, nor why she came to me in the grasses that night and spoke my name.

I do know that I once believed heaven was only clouds and sky. But now I wonder if it might be as well the dark and mysterious sea.

That same night that I walked with Franny on the beach, I returned again, very late, to the shore. Poseidon and I left the cottage around midnight and, with a flashlight, I made my way to the sea grasses where the mermaid had once found me.

I sat there peacefully and looked out across the waters, stroking the head of my beloved dog. I thought about my parents holding hands. I thought about my grandfather carving a small new planet for the world.

And I thought about a girl and her dog,

swimming together forever in that deep blue sea.

Before I left, I stood on a rock and tossed a bottle as far into the water as it would go, letting the tide carry it away. In the bottle was a letter. And it read:

*Dear Anna,*
*Thank you.*
*Daniel*

Cynthia Rylant is the author of more than sixty books, including *Missing May,* a Newbery Medal winner, and the Henry and Mudge stories.